Published by Checkerboard Press, Inc., 30 Vesey Street, New York, New York 10007

MUDPIE, KITT'NVILLE, KITT'NS, and character names are trademarks of Guy Gilchrist Productions, Inc.

ISBN: 1-56288-090-X   Library of Congress Catalog Card Number: 91-2659
Printed in the United States of America   (F1/10)   0 9 8 7 6 5 4 3 2 1

I AM ✫✫✫ HAVING AN EXCELLENT ✫✫✫✫ DAY!

A MUDPIE™ STORY
STRAIGHT·TO·YOU·FROM
KITT'NVILLE · BY
Guy Gilchrist

GUY GILCHRIST

CHECKERBOARD ✫PRESS✫

NEW YORK·NEW YORK

My name is Mudpie. Let me tell you about the day I had. This morning when I went down to the kitchen . . .

the box of my favorite cereal was empty.
There wasn't any in the cupboard either.

So my mom made me *pancakes* instead!
I am having an excellent day.

I went into our garage to get my bicycle and go riding down the street.

But the chain was all droopy.

Then I saw my friend Pawdette riding her skateboard in front of our house. She had a skateboard for me!

I am having an excellent day.

I wanted to play basketball with my friends.
But we couldn't find the basketball.

But we did find a cardboard box full of really neat stuff! So we built a spaceship and blasted off for a quick spin around the universe.

When we came back to earth, my friends had to go home. So I went fishing down at the creek.

Unfortunately, the fish didn't want to be caught.

But I did catch a *turtle, two frogs,* and a *salamander!*

I am having an excellent day!

Later, my friend Banjoey and I
set up camp in my backyard.

We had a tent. We had sleeping bags and flashlights.

We had *rain*. And our tent had leaks!

My dad said we had to come inside.

My mom made us hot chocolate. She said Banjoey and I could camp out in the living room.

This is going to be an excellent night.